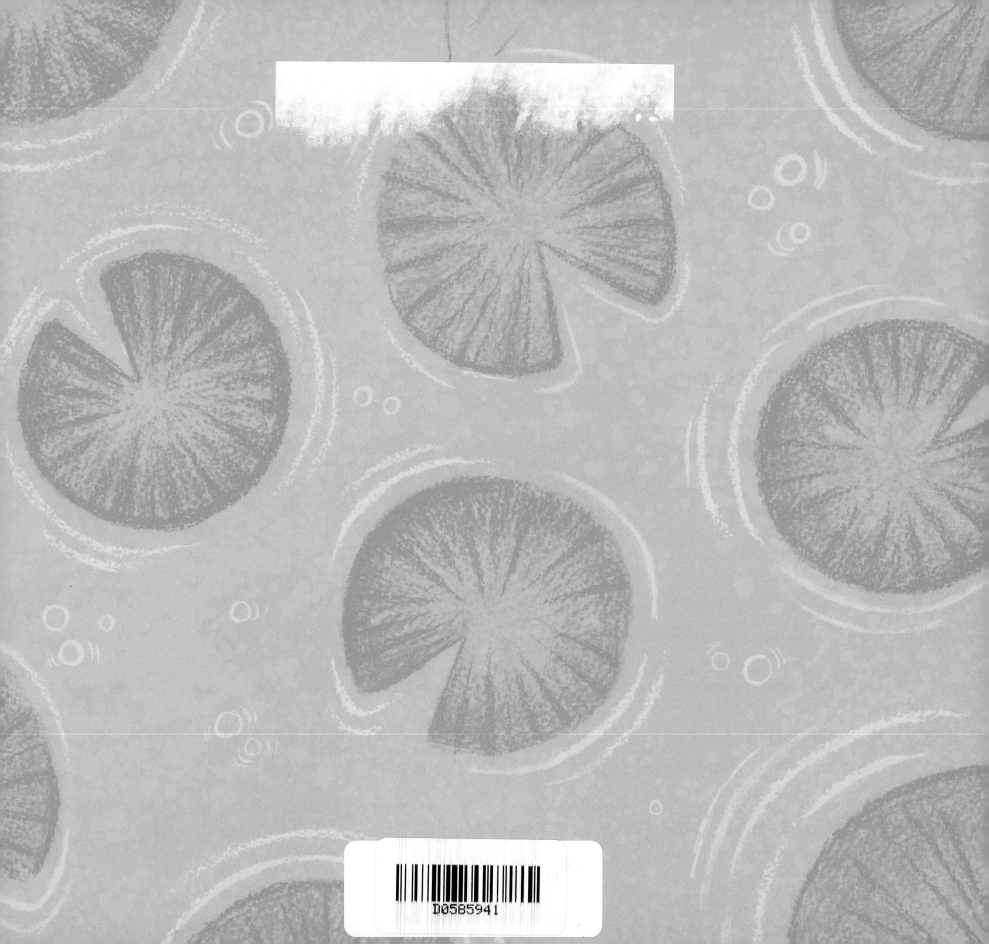

FROG VS TOAD

BEN MANTLE

FOR ALICE AND THE LITTLE
TADPOLE SHE IS GROWING
– B.M.

First published 2021 by Walker Books Ltd, 87 Vauxhall Walk, London SE11 5HJ · Copyright © Ben Mantle · The right of Ben Mantle to be identified as author and illustrator of this work has been asserted by him in accordance with the Copyright, Designs and Patents Act 1988 · This book has been typset in Intensa Fuente and Burbank Big Regular · Printed in China · All rights reserved. No part of this book may be reproduced, transmitted or stored in an information retrieval system in any form or by any means, graphic, electronic or mechanical, including photocopying, taping and recording, without prior written permission from the publisher. · British Library Cataloguing in Publication Data: a catalogue record for this book is available from the British Library · ISBN 978-1-4063-8477-2 (hb) ISBN 978-1-4063-9820-5 (pb) · www.walker.co.uk · 10 9 8 7 6 5 4 3 2 1

WALKER BOOKS
AND SUBSIDIARIES

LONDON · BOSTON · SYDNEY · AUCKLAND

Frog was hiding in the leaves.

His stomach was rumbling.

The juicy fly was almost close enough to taste.

SNAP!

Dinner was served!

SNAP!

Suddenly, another tongue flew out of nowhere!

"HEY! LE' GO. I SAW THE FLY FIRST,"

mumbled Frog.

"**No, ew le' go!**" came the reply.

"THAT ONE IS A TOAD," gasped Frog. "FROGS ARE NOTHING LIKE TOADS!"

"YEAH! I'M NOT A SLIMY FROG," bellowed Toad. The fly saw its chance and buzzed off.

"WAIT ... DID YOU CALL ME **SLIMY**?" croaked Frog. "**WELL, YOU'RE DRY AND LUMPY!**"

Toad was cross.
"**OH, WHY DON'T YOU HOP IT, LONG LEGS!**"

"YOU'RE JUST JEALOUS," teased Frog. "LOOK HOW HIGH I CAN HOP! WORMS HAVE LONGER LEGS THAN YOU ... AND THEY DON'T EVEN HAVE LEGS!"

Frog hopped and hopped.

Toad was upset.

"YEAH, WELL, NOT EVEN A PRINCESS'S KISS COULD TURN **YOU** INTO A PRINCE!" laughed Toad.

"ALL **YOU'RE** GOOD FOR IS A WITCH'S POTION!" Frog shouted back. "AND ...

HOW CAN YOU EVEN SEE ANYTHING WITH THOSE TINY EYES?"

"AT LEAST MINE DON'T SWIVEL ALL OVER THE PLACE," muttered Toad.

"Don't know what you're talking about,"
shrugged Frog.

Frog and Toad couldn't stop squabbling.

"I'M SO MUCH CLEVERER THAN YOU," Frog taunted.

"I'M SO MUCH STRONGER THAN YOU!" bragged Toad.

They continued bickering all the way
to the swamp.

"WELL, TOADS
ABSOLUTELY PONG!"
howled Frog.

"THAT'S NOT FAIR!" bawled Toad.
"YOU KNOW OUR SMELL
STOPS ANYONE EATING US!"

Things were getting a bit lively.

"HUH!" Frog cried, "FROGS ARE JUST BETTER THAN TOADS!"

"NO, TOADS ARE BEST!" boasted Toad.
"So, LA-LA-LA, I'M NOT LISTENING
TO FROGS LIKE YOU ANYMORE."

Frog was ready to burst.
"THAT'S IT! IF YOU SAY
ONE MORE WORD ..."

"**YOU'LL DO WHAT?**" said Toad,
taking a step closer.

Frog had run out of things to say.

SPLAT!

SPLIT! SPLAT! SPLOTCH! SQUELCH!
The frogs and toads were so busy slinging
mud, they didn't even notice ...

someone approaching!

Everyone froze.

Toad squirmed in fright.
"ERR ... THIS FROG STARTED IT.
NOT US TOADS!"

"IT DOESN'T MATTER **WHO** STARTED IT!
FROGS? TOADS? YOU ALL TASTE
THE SAME TO ME, BECAUSE ALL
YOU PEA-BRAINS ARE RELATED.
AND NOW, I'M HUNGRY ..."

"I CAN'T BELIEVE IT—
I'M RELATED TO YOU!"
gasped Frog.

Toad thought for a second,
"YOU KNOW, WE MIGHT BE
DIFFERENT ... BUT ACTUALLY,
YOU'RE ALL RIGHT."

Frog smiled,
"YOU'RE NOT SO BAD YOURSELF!
HEY ... WELCOME TO THE FAMILY!"

"THANKS!" beamed Toad.

Soon, there was a chorus of apologies between the frogs and the toads.

THANKS FOR SHOWING US WE'RE ALL THE SAME, CROCODILE!

"HONESTLY!" said Frog.
"I KNOW," replied Toad.
"SOME FOLK ARE SO TOUCHY."

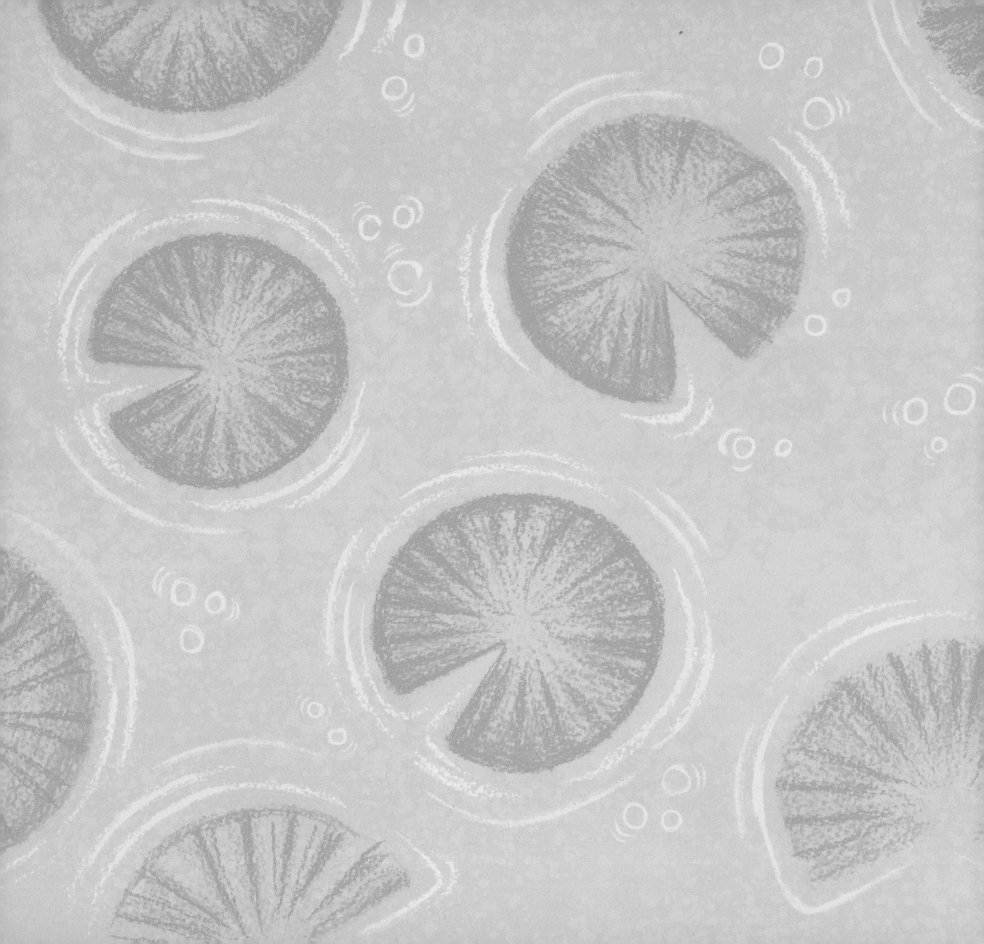